Pebble®

Great Women in History

Florence Nightingale

by Erin Edison

Consulting Editor: Gail Saunders-Smith, PhD

SOUTH HUNTINGTON PUB. LIB.
145 PIDGEON HILL ROAD
HUNTINGTON STA., NY 11746

Pebble Books are published by Capstone Press,
1710 Roe Crest Drive, North Mankato, Minnesota 56003.
www.capstonepub.com

Copyright © 2014 by Capstone Press, a Capstone imprint. All rights reserved.
No part of this publication may be reproduced in whole or in part, or stored in a
retrieval system, or transmitted in any form or by any means, electronic, mechanical,
photocopying, recording, or otherwise, without written permission of the publisher.

Library of Congress Cataloging-in-Publication Data
Edison, Erin.
  Florence Nightingale / by Erin Edison.
     pages cm.—(Pebble books. Great women in history)
  Audience: 6-8.—Audience: K to grade 3.
  Includes bibliographical references and index.
  ISBN 978-1-4765-4214-0 (library binding)—ISBN 978-1-4765-5162-3 (paperback)—
ISBN 978-1-4765-6019-9 (ebook PDF) 1. Nightingale, Florence, 1820-1910—Juvenile
literature. 2. Nurses—Great Britain—Biography. I. Title.
RT37.N5E35 2014
610.73—dc23   2013030094

Editorial Credits
Erika L. Shores, editor; Gene Bentdahl, designer; Marcie Spence, media researcher;
Laura Manthe, production specialist

Photo Credits
Alamy Images: ARGO Images, 4, 10, ClassicStock, 1, David Riley, 20, SuperStock,
8; Corbis: Bettmann, 14; Getty Image: DeAgostini, 6, Hulton Archive, cover, 16, 18,
Universal History Archive, 12

Note to Parents and Teachers

The Great Women in History set supports national social studies
standards related to people and culture. This book describes and
illustrates Florence Nightingale. The images support early readers
in understanding the text. The repetition of words and phrases
helps early readers learn new words. This book also introduces
early readers to subject-specific vocabulary words, which are
defined in the Glossary section. Early readers may need assistance
to read some words and to use the Table of Contents, Glossary,
Read More, Internet Sites, and Index sections of the book.

Printed in the United States of America in North Mankato, Minnesota.
092013   007764CGS14

Table of Contents

Early Life................ 5
Early Work.............. 9
Life's Work 13

Glossary 22
Read More 23
Internet Sites.............23
Critical Thinking Using the
Common Core 24
Index 24

1820

born

Early Life

Florence Nightingale was a nurse who worked to make hospitals safe. She was born in 1820. Florence's family was from England, but they were on vacation in Florence, Italy. Florence was named after the city where she was born.

⬅ Florence (left) with her mother and sister in 1822

1820
born

Florence's father taught her and her sister at home. By age 17, Florence knew she wanted to help people. But she wasn't sure how until 1850. A visit to a hospital helped Florence decide to go to nursing school.

Florence (left) and her sister around 1836

1820 — born

1851 — goes to nursing school

1853 — runs hospital in England

8

Early Work

In 1851 Florence went to Germany to study nursing. By 1853 Florence ran a women's hospital in London. Then in 1854 the Crimean War broke out.

1820 — born
1851 — goes to nursing school
1853 — runs hospital in England

British soldiers were fighting in the country of Turkey. The British badly needed nurses to care for hurt soldiers. Florence gathered 38 other nurses and went to help.

1854-1856
helps soldiers in Crimean War

1820 born

1851 goes to nursing school

1853 runs hospital in England

Life's Work

Florence arrived to find the war hospital dirty and full of germs. Germs cause infections. More soldiers died from infections than from war wounds. Florence worked to make the hospital clean and safe.

1854–1856
helps soldiers in Crimean War

1820 — born

1851 — goes to nursing school

1853 — runs hospital in England

At the war hospital, Florence was known as "The Lady with the Lamp." Florence walked the hospital hallways each night with a lamp. She helped anyone who needed care.

1854-1856
helps soldiers in Crimean War

Letter from Miss FLORENCE NIGHTINGALE.

Dec 16/96
10, SOUTH STREET,
PARK LANE W.

Dear Duke of Westminster

Good speed to your noble effort in favour of District Nurses for town & country; and in Commemoration of our Queen who cares for all.

We look upon the District Nurse, if she is what she should be, & if we give her the training she should have, as the Great civilizer of the poor. training as well as nursing them out of ill health into good health (Health Missioners), out of drink into self control, but all without preaching, without patronizing — as friends in sympathy.

But let them hold the Standard high as Nurses

Pray be sure I will try to help all I can, tho' that be small, here I will with your leave let you know.

Pray believe me your Grace's faithful servant

Florence Nightingale

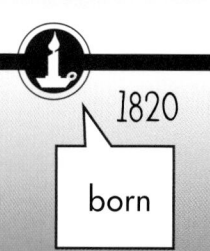

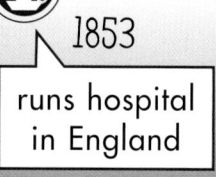

1820 — born

1851 — goes to nursing school

1853 — runs hospital in England

Florence returned to London after the war. She wrote letters to leaders in Great Britain. She told them about the importance of clean and safe hospitals.

1854-1856
helps soldiers in Crimean War

1820 — born

1851 — goes to nursing school

1853 — runs hospital in England

18

In 1860 Florence started a school to train nurses. She wrote letters about nursing to students. She also wrote books about clean hospitals and proper nursing care.

◀ Florence, seated in center, with a group of nurses in 1886

1854-1856
helps soldiers in Crimean War

1820 born

1851 goes to nursing school

1853 runs hospital in England

In 1870 Florence helped start the British Red Cross. This group helps people after wars and disasters. Florence died in London in 1910. She is remembered for making hospitals cleaner and safer for everyone.

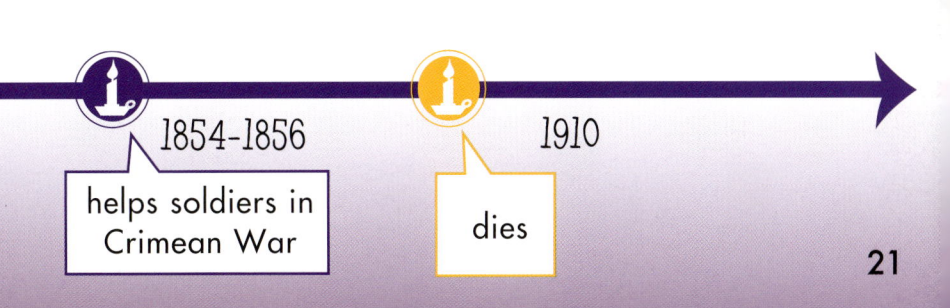

1854-1856
helps soldiers in Crimean War

1910
dies

Glossary

Crimean War—a war lasting from 1853 to 1865 in which England and France stopped Russia from taking part of the Ottoman Empire; this area is now Turkey

disaster—an event that causes much damage or suffering

germ—a very small living thing that can cause disease

infection—an illness caused by germs

soldier—a person who is in the military

wound—an injury or a cut

Read More

Ready, Dee. *Nurses Help.* Our Community Helpers. North Mankato, Minn.: Capstone Press, 2013.

Ridley, Sarah. *Florence Nightingale—And a New Age of Nursing.* History Makers. Mankato, Minn.: Sea-to-Sea Publications, 2013.

Zeiger, Jennifer. *What Do They Do? Nurses.* Community Connections. Ann Arbor, Mich.: Cherry Lake Pub., 2010.

Internet Sites

FactHound offers a safe, fun way to find Internet sites related to this book. All of the sites on FactHound have been researched by our staff.

Here's all you do:

Visit *www.facthound.com*

Type in this code: 9781476542140

Check out projects, games and lots more at **www.capstonekids.com**

Critical Thinking Using the Common Core

1. How did working in a war hospital help Florence learn about germs? (Key Ideas and Details)

2. After the war, Florence did everything she could to spread information about the importance of clean hospitals. Do you think her teaching still has an impact on hospitals today? Explain why or why not. (Integration of Knowledge and Ideas)

Index

birth, 5
British Red Cross, 21
Crimean War, 9, 11
death, 21
family, 5, 7
father, 7
Florence, Italy, 5
germs, 13
hospitals, 5, 7, 9, 13, 15, 17, 19, 21
infections, 13
"The Lady with the Lamp," 15
letters, 17, 19
London, England, 9, 17, 21
nursing schools 7, 9, 19
sister, 7

Word Count: 281
Grade: 1
Early-Intervention Level: 23

9/5/99

DISCARD